Milly Molly®

B O O K S

This Milly, Molly book belongs to

For my grandchildren

Thomas, Harry, Ella and Madeleine.

Milly, Molly and the Sunhat

Copyright © Milly Molly Books, 2002

Gill Pittar and Cris Morrell assert the moral right to
be recognised as the author and illustrator of this work.

Published by
Milly Molly Books
P O Box 539
Gisborne, New Zealand
email: books@millymolly.com

Printed by Rhythm Consolidated Berhad, Malaysia

ISBN: 1-877297-23-2

10   9   8   7   6   5   4   3   2   1

Milly, Molly
and the
Sunhat

"We may look different
but we feel the same."

It was summer again.

Milly and Molly had just finished their picnic when a big, brown, straw sunhat blew along the beach towards them.

"I wonder who owns it?" said Milly.
"Come on, let's find out," suggested Molly.

They didn't need to ask the two boys
digging bunkers in the sand. They could just
see the tops of their sunhats.
It wasn't theirs.

They didn't need to ask the fisherman sitting on a rock. He had his hat pulled tightly down over his ears. It wasn't his.

They didn't need to ask the lady filling her basket with seaweed. She had her hand firmly on the top of her hat. It wasn't hers.

They didn't need to ask the little girls building castles in the sand. They had their hats tied under their chins. It wasn't theirs.

They didn't need to ask the sunbathers
with busy feet. They were under a striped
umbrella. It couldn't be theirs.

They didn't need to ask the old man with
a knobbly stick. He had wild hair escaping
from under his beanie. It wasn't his.

They didn't need to ask the windsurfers.
They had zinc on their noses and wind
in their ears. It wouldn't be theirs.

But what about the four snorklers?
There were four pairs of boots but
only three sunhats!

Milly and Molly slipped the big, brown, straw sunhat under the fourth pair of boots and ran all the way back to their picnic basket.

They passed lots of people
on the way home, some with sunhats
and some without.
"I hope we found the right owner,"
said Milly.

"Look," cried Molly. "We did."

B O O K S

Other picture books in the Milly, Molly values series include:

- Milly Molly's Monday   ISBN 0-9582208-0-8

- Milly Molly and What Was That?   ISBN 0-9582208-1-6

- Milly Molly and Jimmy's Seeds   ISBN 0-9582208-2-4

- Milly Molly and Beefy   ISBN 0-9582208-3-2

- Milly, Molly and Taffy Bogle   ISBN 0-9582208-4-0

- Milly, Molly and Oink   ISBN 0-9582208-5-9

- Milly, Molly and BushBob   ISBN 0-9582208-6-7

- Milly, Molly and Grandpa's Oak Tree   ISBN 0-9582208-7-5

- Milly, Molly and Alf   ISBN 1-877297-24-0

- Milly, Molly and Aunt Maude   ISBN 1-877297-25-9

- Milly, Molly and Sock Heaven   ISBN 1-877297-26-7

- Milly, Molly and the Secret Scarves   ISBN 1-877297-27-5

- Milly, Molly and the Mountain   ISBN 1-877297-28-3

- Milly, Molly and Different Dads   ISBN 1-877297-29-1

- Milly and Molly Go Camping   ISBN 1-877297-30-5

w w w . m i l l y m o l l y . c o m